TRAPPED FOR THE HOLIDAYS

E.B. FOX

CHAPTER 1

The wind howls, whipping icy snowflakes against my numb cheeks as I stumble through the growing drifts, my boots sinking into the relentless white. My car sits uselessly behind me, the engine dead, abandoning me to the mercy of the storm. Desperation claws at my throat.

This is just my luck. I swear I've got the shittiest luck of anyone on this godforsaken planet.

I walk for what feels like forever, and my panic starts to grow.

I have to find shelter, or I'm going to die out here.

Finally, there's light at the end of the tunnel.

There. Through the swirling flakes, I spot a

light glimmering faintly in the distance. A cabin.

I nearly sob with relief.

Propelled by sheer force of will, I push onward, my stiff legs moving mechanically until at last I'm climbing creaking wooden steps onto a small porch. Breathless, I pound on the door, silently pleading. *Please, please...*

The door wrenches open. I blink up at the tall silhouette looming before me, backlit by the glow of a fire. A man's hard face appears as he steps into the light. Arresting. Unforgiving. His icy blue eyes rake over me, his expression inscrutable.

Holy fuck, this dude looks scary, but I have to take my chances with him because what other choice do I have?

"I—my car broke down," I stammer, my voice trembling from more than just cold. "I saw your light..."

He regards me in stony silence for a long, assessing moment. The intensity of his stare unnerves me.

Just as I'm certain he'll turn me away, he steps back, motioning me inside with a curt nod. Weak with relief and trepidation, I cross the threshold into his cabin. The heavy door closes with an ominous thud behind me.

The heat from the crackling fireplace envelops me, a stark contrast to the chill emanating from my reluctant host. He prowls past me, a caged predator in this confined space. Every movement is coiled with restrained power, setting my nerves on edge.

"Thank you," I manage, my words sounding small and inadequate. "I'm Eliza. Eliza Grey."

He pauses, his broad shoulders tensing slightly. "Ronan Black," he replies, his deep voice scraping over me like gravel. He doesn't offer anything more, leaving me to fill the charged silence.

I take in my surroundings, seeking distraction from his unsettling presence. The cabin is sparse but strangely beautiful, with deep shadows playing across the rustic furniture. Haunting landscapes adorn the walls, the brushstrokes raw and visceral. They draw me in, whispering of untold stories.

"Did you paint these?" I ask softly, momentarily forgetting my unease. "They're incredible."

Ronan's jaw clenches, a muscle ticking

beneath the stubble. "Yes," he says shortly, offering no further elaboration. His gaze follows mine to the paintings, a flicker of some indecipherable emotion passing over his features.

The air thickens with unspoken things, the crackle of the fire the only sound. I can't shake the feeling that I've stumbled into something far more complex than a simple shelter from the storm.

"You can stay the night," Ronan finally says, his tone making it clear it's not a choice. "But you leave in the morning."

I nod, my throat suddenly dry. "Of course. I appreciate your hospitality."

His lips twist into a humorless smile. "Don't mistake this for hospitality, Miss Grey. You're an inconvenience, nothing more."

The words sting, but I lift my chin, refusing to cower. "An inconvenience that won't overstay her welcome, I assure you."

Something flashes in his eyes, gone too quickly to interpret. He studies me for a weighted moment before turning abruptly and stalking off.

Okay then. I guess I'll find my own way to a room?

I watch Ronan's retreating back until he

disappears into the shadows of the cabin, leaving me alone in the flickering firelight. The weight of my exhaustion presses down on me, and I sway on my feet. I need to find a place to rest before I collapse.

Steeling myself, I venture deeper into the cabin, my eyes adjusting to the dim light. The floorboards creak beneath my boots, echoing in the stillness. A narrow hallway stretches before me, lined with closed doors that seem to guard their secrets.

I pause at the first door, my hand hovering over the knob. Would it be too presumptuous to open it? Ronan didn't exactly give me a tour. But he also didn't specify where I should stay. Taking a steadying breath, I turn the knob and push the door open.

The room is small but clean, with a single bed tucked against the wall. A patchwork quilt covers the mattress, its faded colors telling stories of its own. I step inside, the door clicking shut behind me. The silence wraps around me like a cocoon, broken only by the distant howl of the wind outside.

I sink down onto the bed, the springs creaking beneath my weight. My body aches with a bone-deep weariness, the events of the night catching up to me. I should probably try to find a blanket or something to ward off the chill, but I can't summon the energy to move.

As I lie there, staring up at the rough-hewn ceiling, my thoughts drift to Ronan. His cold demeanor, his piercing gaze, the way he carries himself like a man haunted by demons I can only imagine. There's a story there, hidden beneath the surface. The journalist in me itches to uncover it.

But I'm not here to pry into his secrets. I'm here to survive the night and be on my way come morning. Simple as that.

Sleep tugs at me, my eyelids growing heavy. I burrow deeper into the quilt, its musty scent oddly comforting. The last thing I remember before drifting off is the sound of the wind whipping against the cabin walls and the fleeting image of Ronan's face, etched with shadows and mystery.

———

I wake with a start, disoriented and shivering. The room is dark, the fire in the main room reduced to embers. I must have slept for hours.

I sit up, rubbing my eyes, trying to gather my bearings.

Thirst claws at my throat. I need water. Slowly, I ease myself off the bed, my muscles protesting the movement. I fumble my way to the door and step out into the hallway, the floorboards cold beneath my sock-clad feet.

The cabin is quiet, almost unnaturally so. I strain my ears, listening for any sign of Ronan, but hear nothing. I pad softly down the hallway, my heart beating a little faster with each step. The main room is empty, the dying firelight casting eerie shadows on the walls. I spot a kitchen off to the side and make my way toward it, hoping to find a glass of water to soothe my parched throat.

As I enter the kitchen, I freeze. Ronan is there, his back to me as he stands at the counter. The muscles of his shoulders are taut beneath his black t-shirt, tension radiating from his frame. He doesn't turn, but I know he senses my presence.

"I...I was just looking for some water," I say, my voice sounding too loud in the stillness.

He reaches up to a cupboard, retrieving a glass. The clink of it against the counter is jarring. He fills it from the tap, the water splashing against the sides. Then, he turns, holding the glass out to me, his expression unreadable.

"Thanks," I murmur, taking the glass from him. Our fingers brush, and a jolt of awareness shoots through me. His skin is warm, a contrast to his icy demeanor.

I take a sip, the cool water a relief to my dry mouth. Ronan watches me, his gaze intense and searching. The silence stretches between us, heavy with unspoken questions.

"Why are you here, Ms. Grey?" he asks finally, his voice low and rough. "Out here in the middle of nowhere in a snowstorm?"

I swallow, considering my answer. "I needed to get away," I say simply. "To find somewhere quiet to sort out my thoughts."

His lips curve into a sardonic smile. "And you thought a remote cabin in a blizzard was the perfect place for that?"

I meet his gaze, refusing to be cowed. "I didn't exactly plan on the blizzard part. And I wasn't sure where I was going. I was just passing through here."

Something flickers in his eyes, a hint of begrudging respect, perhaps. "No, I suppose you didn't."

He turns away, bracing his hands on the counter. The lines of his body are rigid, as if he's barely holding himself in check. I wonder what it would take to break through that control.

"What about you, Ronan?" I ask softly. "Why are you here, all alone in the middle of nowhere?"

His shoulders stiffen, and for a moment, I think he won't answer. But then, he lets out a slow breath. "Penance, maybe. Or punishment. Take your pick."

My heart clenches at the raw pain in his voice. There's a story there, a wound that hasn't healed. I ache to know more, to understand the man beneath the hard exterior.

But one look into his hard eyes lets me know that asking wouldn't be a good idea.

Instead, I swallow.

"Get some sleep, Ms. Grey. We'll get you sorted in the morning."

And with that, I'm effectively dismissed.

I know better than to overstay my welcome. He's already made it clear I'm an inconvenience.

I can't wait to get the hell out of here come morning.

CHAPTER 2

gasp awake the next morning, my heart pounding in my chest. For a moment, I'm disoriented, unsure of where I am. Then it all comes rushing back—the snowstorm, my car breaking down, the imposing cabin in the woods.

Ronan.

I sit up, the patchwork quilt falling away from my shoulders. Pale light filters through the small window, casting a soft glow across the room. It must be morning, but the light seems muted, subdued. I frown, slipping out of bed and padding over to the window.

What I see makes my breath catch in my throat. Snow blankets everything, a thick, unbroken expanse of white stretching as far as the eye can see. It's piled high against the cabin, reaching halfway up the window panes. The storm must have raged on through the night, dumping an impossible amount of snow.

My heart sinks as the realization hits me. There's no way I'm going anywhere today. I'm stuck here, in this cabin, with a man who clearly wants nothing to do with me.

Fantastic.

With a sigh, I turn away from the window, running a hand through my sleep-tousled hair. I might as well face the music. Steeling myself, I venture out into the hallway, the floorboards creaking softly beneath my bare feet. The cabin is quiet, save for the faint crackle of a fire in the main room. I follow the sound, my stomach twisting with nerves.

As I step into the room, I'm greeted by the sight of Ronan's broad back as he stands before the hearth, poking at the flames with an iron poker. He's dressed in a dark green flannel and worn jeans that hug his lean hips. His dark hair is slightly mussed, as if he's been running his fingers through it. Something about the sight makes my pulse quicken.

He stiffens as I enter, clearly sensing my presence. Slowly, he turns, his icy blue eyes locking onto mine. His jaw is set, his expression unreadable.

"Sleep well?" he asks, his voice a low rumble.

I nod, swallowing past the sudden dryness in my throat. "Yes, thank you."

He grunts in acknowledgment, turning back to the fire. I hover uncertainly, unsure of what to do with myself. My gaze drifts around the room, taking in the rustic decor—the worn leather couch, the rough-hewn wooden beams, the antlers mounted on the wall. It's masculine and rugged, just like the man who inhabits it.

"There's coffee in the kitchen," Ronan says abruptly, jerking his chin towards the adjoining room. "Help yourself."

Grateful for the reprieve, I hurry into the kitchen. The rich aroma of coffee fills my

The rich aroma of coffee fills my nostrils as I enter the kitchen, a welcome respite from the tension crackling between Ronan and me. I spot the pot on the counter, steam curling invitingly from its spout. Grabbing a mug from the dish rack, I pour myself a generous amount, relishing the warmth that seeps into my palms.

I take a sip, the hot liquid soothing my frayed nerves. As I lower the mug, my gaze falls on the window above the sink. The view beyond is a stark white, the snow piled so high it obscures the bottom pane. A shiver runs through me, and it has nothing to do with the temperature.

Footsteps approach behind me, heavy and measured. I stiffen, my fingers tightening around the mug. Ronan's presence fills the small kitchen, his body heat radiating against my back. I force myself to turn, meeting his penetrating gaze head-on.

"We're snowed in," he says bluntly, his voice rough as gravel. "Looks like you'll be staying put for a while."

My heart sinks, even as a traitorous thrill hums through my veins. Being trapped here with Ronan, in this secluded cabin, feels dangerous in more ways than one. I lick my suddenly dry lips, noticing how his eyes track the movement.

"How long do you think it will take to clear?" I ask, hating the breathless quality of my voice.

He shrugs, the motion rippling through his broad shoulders. "Could be days. Depends on how much more snow we get."

Days. Alone with this enigmatic, brooding

man who both unnerves and intrigues me. The prospect is as thrilling as it is terrifying. I take another sip of coffee, needing the scalding liquid to ground me.

"Is there anything I can do to help?" I offer, grasping for some sense of normalcy. "I don't want to be a burden."

Something flickers in Ronan's eyes, gone too quickly for me to decipher. "You're not a burden," he says, his voice low. "But there's not much to be done. We just have to wait it out."

Wait it out. The words hang heavily in the air between us, laden with unspoken possibilities. My pulse thrums as Ronan's gaze rakes over me, lingering on the curve of my neck, the swell of my breasts beneath my sweater. Heat coils low in my belly, a traitorous response to his blatant perusal.

"I should check the generator," he says abruptly, tearing his eyes away. "Make sure we have enough fuel to last."

He brushes past me, his arm grazing mine, leaving a trail of goosebumps in his wake. I release a shaky breath, watching him disappear down the hall.

What the hell have I gotten myself into?

CHAPTER 3

Snow falls furiously, big, fat flakes. I watch the storm unleash its fury, mirroring the turmoil raging within me. Questions swirl in my mind like wind-tossed leaves, each one a mystery I ache to unravel. Who is Ronan Black, really?

I turn away from the window, the weight of uncertainty pressing down on my shoulders. The dimly lit room feels suddenly suffocating, the air thick. I need to move, to breathe.

I feel *trapped.*

I step into the corridor, the floorboards creaking softly beneath my bare feet. The warm glow of the lamps casts flickering shadows on the walls, dancing to a silent rhythm. Each step I take is tentative, as if the very walls are listening, guarding their secrets with a watchful vigilance.

As I move through the hallway, the scent of aged wood envelops me. My fingertips trail along the rough textures. The cabin feels alive, pulsing with an energy I can't quite define. It's both inviting and unsettling, a contradiction that mirrors the man who calls it home.

Ronan Black. The name whispers through my thoughts, a dark caress that sends shivers down my spine. He is an enigma, a puzzle I yearn to solve. In the brief moments we've shared, I've glimpsed a depth in his piercing blue eyes, a haunting beauty that speaks of hidden sorrows and untold truths.

I pause, my heart racing in the stillness. The storm outside rages on, the wind howling like a mournful chorus. In this moment, I am acutely aware of my isolation, of the danger I could be in here with a man I scarcely know.

I come across a closed door, and curiosity burns within me. Heart beating in my chest, I turn the doorknob, but it resists.

Locked.

"Find anything interesting?"

Ronan's voice cuts through the silence like a knife, startling me. I jump and spin around with a gasp, my heart pounding in my chest as I meet his gaze. His eyes are dark, stormy with an emotion I can't quite decipher. Anger, perhaps, or something more complex, more *primal*.

I feel the stinging shame of guilt at being caught red-handed.

"I was just..." I falter, the words sticking in my throat. "I didn't mean to pry."

"Didn't you?" He takes a step closer, his presence overwhelming in the narrow corridor. "You're a journalist, Eliza. Prying is what you do."

My eyes widen as I sputter, "How—how do you know that?"

"I'm not without my resources," he growls as he glares down at me. "Why are you really here?" he asks me suspiciously.

And then, my investigative journalist's instincts kick in. He's angry because he thinks I'm here to find out something about him.

Which indicates he's hiding something he doesn't want found out.

The accusation stings, but I refuse to back down. "And what about you, Ronan? What are you hiding behind that door?"

His jaw clenches, a muscle twitching

beneath the surface. "Some things are better left unknown."

I square my shoulders, meeting his stare with a defiance that surprises even me. "Try me."

The air between us crackles with tension, a palpable force that threatens to ignite at any moment. Ronan's eyes bore into mine, searching, probing, as if trying to uncover the secrets of my own soul. I feel exposed, vulnerable, but I refuse to look away.

"Be careful what you wish for, Eliza," he warns, his voice low and dangerous. "The truth can be a heavy burden to bear."

I swallow hard, my mouth suddenly dry. "I'm not afraid of the truth."

He laughs then, a harsh, mirthless sound that echoes through the empty hallways. "You should be."

With that, he turns and walks away, leaving me alone once more in the shadows. I watch him go, my heart racing, my mind reeling with questions I'm not sure I want the answers to. But even as fear curls in the pit of my stomach, I know that I can't turn back now.

I turn away from the locked door, my heart still pounding in the aftermath of our heated exchange. The air feels thick with unspoken words, and I can't shake the feeling that we're standing on the edge of something dangerous, something that could consume us both if we're not careful.

I make my way back to the main room, the fire in the hearth casting flickering shadows on the walls. Ronan stands by the window, his back to me, his silhouette etched against the raging storm outside. The tension between us is palpable, a living, breathing thing that fills the space and steals the oxygen from my lungs.

"Why are you really here, Eliza?" he asks, his voice cutting through the silence like a knife.

"I told you, my car broke down. You're the first place I stumbled across after nearly one freezing hour of walking," I saw with obvious irritation in my voice. "Believe me or not. I might be a journalist, but I didn't come here to investigate you. Hell, I don't even know who you are, but your obvious conclusion that I'm here looking for some story tells me there is one."

He turns to face me then, his blue eyes piercing in the dim light. "And you just happened to stumble upon my cabin, in the middle of nowhere, in the dead of winter?"

I meet his gaze, refusing to back down. "I don't believe in coincidences, Ronan. But I also don't believe in prying into other people's lives."

He takes a step closer, and I feel the heat of his body, the intensity of his presence. "And yet, here you are, trying to unlock my secrets."

I stand my ground, even as my heart races in my chest. "I'm not trying to unlock anything. I'm just trying to understand."

"Understand what?" he demands, his voice low and rough.

"You," I whisper, the word hanging in the air between us like a confession.

For a moment, he says nothing, his eyes searching mine as if he's trying to read my very thoughts. Then, slowly, he reaches out and brushes a strand of hair from my face, his touch sending shivers down my spine.

He's so close I can feel his breath warm against my skin.

I close my eyes, leaning into his touch even as my mind screams at me to pull away.

He cups my face in his hands, his gaze intense and hungry. We stare at one another.

And then his lips are on mine. He growls,

and I feel that rumble deep down in my own soul.

His arms tighten around me, pulling me flush against him. I feel his erection, huge and instant pressing into my stomach, and the answering throb between my legs has me instantly wet.

His kiss is rough, like that of an untamed animal. Holy fuck, I've *never* been kissed like this before.

Ronan's hands slide down my back, his touch electric against my skin. I arch into him, my fingers tangling in his hair, pulling him closer, desperate to eliminate any space between us. The kiss deepens, a clash of tongues and teeth, a dance of dominance and submission that leaves me breathless and aching for more.

He breaks away, his lips trailing a path of fire down my neck, his breath hot against my ear. "Tell me to stop," he murmurs, his voice rough with desire.

I tremble at his words, at the raw need that underscores them. A part of me knows I should push him away, but I can't.

So, I don't so anything.

He growls and keeps kissing me, his lips

trailing over my throat, leaving heat in their wake.

Finally, I wrench myself away, gasping for air.

The room seems to spin as I pull away, my breath coming in short, ragged gasps. The firelight dances across Ronan's face, casting shadows that emphasize the sharp angles of his cheekbones, the intensity of his gaze. My heart pounds in my chest, a relentless rhythm that echoes the chaos of my thoughts.

Ronan steps back, his expression guarded once more, as if he's suddenly realized the gravity of what just transpired between us. He runs a hand through his disheveled hair, his eyes darting away from mine, and I sense a flicker of vulnerability beneath his stoic exterior.

I study him, desperate to unravel the enigma that is Ronan Black. The lines of his face tell a story, one of pain and loss, of secrets buried deep within. I yearn to reach out, to trace the contours of his jaw, to smooth away the furrow between his brows, but I hesitate, unsure if I'm ready to cross that invisible line.

"Ronan," I whisper, my voice barely audible

above the crackling of the fire. "Talk to me. Please."

He meets my gaze then, and I'm struck by the depth of emotion swirling in those blue eyes. It's as if a storm rages within him, a tempest of conflicting desires and unspoken truths. He opens his mouth, then closes it again, as if the words are too heavy, too painful to voice.

The silence stretches between us, thick with unspoken questions and unresolved tension. I take a tentative step forward, my hand reaching out to him, but he flinches away, as if my touch might burn him.

"No," he says, his voice rough with emotion.

And with that, he turns and strides from the room, leaving me alone with the ghosts of our shared passion and the bitter taste of rejection on my tongue.

I sink onto the worn leather couch, my legs suddenly weak, my mind reeling from the intensity of what just happened. The room feels colder now, the shadows deeper, as if Ronan's absence has stolen the warmth from the very air.

I close my eyes, trying to make sense of the tumult within me.

I retreat to my room, my mind a tempest of swirling thoughts and emotions. The memory of Ronan's kiss lingers on my lips, a phantom sensation that refuses to fade. I close the door behind me, leaning against it for support as I try to steady my racing heart.

The storm outside rages on, the wind howling like a tortured soul, rattling the windows with its relentless fury. I make my way to the bed, sinking down onto the soft mattress as I stare unseeingly at the shadows that dance across the walls, cast by the flickering light of a single candle.

I close my eyes, but sleep eludes me, chased away by the turmoil within. Ronan's face swims before me, those piercing blue eyes that seem to see straight into my soul, the hard planes of his jaw, the sensual curve of his lips. I can still feel the heat of his body pressed against mine, the raw power of his kiss, the way it ignited a fire deep within me.

But beneath the desire, there is something else, a whisper of pain, a hint of secrets left unspoken. The vulnerability I glimpsed in those fleeting moments haunts me, tugging at my heart, urging me to unravel the mystery that surrounds him.

As I finally drift into a restless slumber, my dreams are filled with shadows and secrets, a labyrinth of unanswered questions and unspoken truths. Ronan's presence permeates every corner of my subconscious, a dark and alluring figure that beckons me closer, even as a part of me yearns to run.

In the depths of my dreams, I find myself standing before that locked door once more, the handle cold and unyielding beneath my touch. But this time, when I turn, it is not Ronan who stands behind me, but a figure cloaked in shadows, a specter of the past that reaches out with ghostly fingers, threatening to drag me into the abyss.

I awaken with a start, my heart pounding, my skin slick with sweat. The storm has quieted, but the silence that settles over the cabin is heavy with unspoken secrets. As I lie there, trying to catch my breath, I know that I am standing on the edge of something profound, a precipice from which there may be no return.

But even as fear courses through my veins, I cannot deny the inexorable pull that draws me towards Ronan, the need to uncover the truth that lies behind those haunted eyes.

CHAPTER 4

Moonlight spills through the window, casting eerie shadows as I pad softly down the hallway, throat parched. The old floorboards creak beneath my bare feet. As I near Ronan's door, a sound stops me cold.

Guttural moans, pained and feral, emanate from inside his room. My heart races, pulse pounding in my ears. Is he hurt? In trouble? I press my palm to the door, the dark wood cool against my skin. Another groan, this one deeper, more primal. I have to see if he's okay.

Slowly, I turn the doorknob, easing the door open a crack. Candlelight flickers within, illuminating a sight that steals my breath. Ronan lays sprawled on his bed, completely naked.

One hand grips the sheets while the other pumps furiously up and down his rigid shaft. Sweat glistens on his muscular chest, his head thrown back in tortured ecstasy.

I should look away. Close the door and pretend I saw nothing. But I'm frozen, transfixed by the erotic scene before me. The flexing of his abs, the power in his strokes. Desire coils hot and heavy low in my belly. Seeing him like this, so raw and unguarded, only intensifies the forbidden attraction simmering between us.

As if sensing my presence, his eyes snap open, locking onto mine. Instead of anger or embarrassment, a feral hunger blazes in those icy blue depths. A growl rumbles from his chest.

In one fluid motion, Ronan is on his feet, cum flying from his cock as he strides towards me, his erection still hard and imposing. His eyes burn with a fire I've never seen before, terrifying and irresistible in equal measure. His hand fists in my hair, yanking my mouth to his, and I moan into the brutal kiss. His other hand grips my hip, dragging me against him, our naked bodies pressed together. I can feel his want for me, hot and demanding, and it spurs my arousal even further.

His lips are an onslaught, claiming and possessive, and I arch into him, craving more. His tongue invades my mouth, exploring every corner, tasting me the way I've fantasized he would. The kiss is messy and desperate, filled with the pent-up desire we've both been denying.

Finally, he pulls away, his breath ragged as he studies me with those icy blue eyes. "You don't know what you're getting into, little girl," he growls. "I'm not a man who settles for simple or sweet. I demand everything."

A shiver runs down my spine, but I refuse to back down. "I'm not looking for simple or sweet."

With a growl of pure male possession, Ronan lunges forward, seizing my wrist and yanking me into the room. The door slams shut behind me as he crushes his lips to mine in another searing kiss. All rational thought flees, consumed by the inferno raging between us. His tongue plunders my mouth, claiming me, possessed me.

"Last warning, little girl," he rasps against my lips. His large hands grip my waist, holding me flush against his hard body. I can feel every ripple of muscle, every inch of his arousal. "I'm not a gentle lover, Eliza."

His words send a shiver down my spine, igniting a primal need deep within me. I've spent so long burying my desires, denying the shadows lurking in my soul. But with Ronan, I long to embrace them. To surrender to the dark passions he stirs to life.

"I'm not afraid," I breathe, my voice barely above a whisper.

His breath comes out in harsh croaks, and his eyes hold a promise of pleasure edged with pain. His fingers tangle in my hair, tugging my head back to expose the column of my throat. "You will be," he growls before nipping sharply at my pulse point.

I gasp, the sting only fueling the ache building between my thighs. Ronan trails a path of hot, open-mouthed kisses along my jaw, my neck, his stubble abrading my sensitive skin. Each scrape of his teeth, each swirl of his tongue, sends bolts of electricity straight to my core.

Impatient hands tear at my clothes, the fabric giving way like gossamer. Cool air kisses my fevered flesh, pebbling my nipples into aching buds. Ronan drinks in the sight of me, his gaze molten with hunger. "Exquisite," he rumbles. "Now, get on the bed."

Robbed of speech, I merely nod, moving on trembling legs to obey his command. The sheets are still warm from his body, the musky scent of his arousal filling my lungs. I barely have a moment to settle before Ronan is on me, pinning my wrists above my head.

"Keep them there," he orders, his tone brooking no argument. Slowly, he maps the curves of my body, callused fingertips igniting sparks in their wake. He palms my breasts, kneading the soft swells before pinching the puckered peaks. I arch into his touch, a low moan escaping my lips.

"So responsive," he purrs, satisfaction lacing his words. "I'm going to unravel you, Eliza Grey. Shatter you into a million pieces and remake you as I see fit." His hand drifts lower, skimming over the quivering plane of my stomach to the apex of my thighs. "And when I'm done, you'll be ruined for any other man."

My mind reels at his provocative promise, even as my body pulses with anticipation. There's a dark thrill in surrendering control to someone like Ronan.

I watch, breath suspended, as he settles

between my splayed legs, shouldering them wider. The first swipe of his tongue through my slick folds has me keening, my hands fisting in his hair. He licks a slow, deliberate stripe from my entrance to the sensitive bundle of nerves at the apex, savoring my essence like a rare delicacy.

"Divine," he mumbles into my flesh, the vibrations adding an erotic counterpoint to his skillful ministrations. Ronan laps at me, delving deep before focusing on my clit with devastating precision. Two thick fingers enter me, curling in a come-hither motion that has me seeing stars.

My hips undulate shamelessly, chasing my peak even as he pushes me towards it. The pressure inside me builds, hot and sharp and overwhelming. "That's it," he coaxes darkly, his ice-blue eyes searing into mine. "Come for me, Eliza. Drench my face with your juices."

His filthy words are my undoing. I shatter with a ragged scream, back bowing off the bed as ecstasy overtakes me. Ronan doesn't relent, wringing out every last tremor and aftershock until I lay spent and boneless among the tangled sheets.

But he's not done with me.

Before I can catch my breath, Ronan is crawling up my body, his hard length dragging along my oversensitized flesh. He looms over me, a dark god ready to claim his sacrifice. "I'm nowhere near finished with you," he rasps, his voice rough with need. "By the time I'm done, you won't remember your own name."

He notches himself at my entrance, his tip barely breaching me. I'm still fluttering from my orgasm, but I crave the stretch, the burn of his possession. Ronan teases me with shallow thrusts, his jaw clenched tight as he fights for control. "Beg me for it, Eliza," he demands. "I want to hear how much you need my cock splitting you open."

A whimper escapes me, my pride warring with my desperation. But the dark hunger in his eyes decimates my defenses. "Please, Ronan," I gasp, my nails raking down his sweat-slicked back. "I need you inside me. I need you to fuck me until I can't walk, can't think beyond the feel of you pounding into me."

A low, feral sound rumbles from his chest, and then he's slamming home, burying himself to the hilt in one brutal thrust. I cry out at the sudden invasion, my body struggling to accommodate his girth. But there's no respite, no chance to adjust as he sets a punishing rhythm, his hips snapping against mine with ruthless precision.

The pleasure-pain is exquisite, each forceful drive hitting something deep inside me. Ronan fills me, completes me in a way I've never known. It's frightening, this dark craving, this primal need he's unleashed. But there's no denying the rightness of his body moving over me, inside me.

He shifts, hooking my legs over his shoulders, the new angle allowing him to plunge even deeper. His pelvis grinds against my clit with each thrust, sending shockwaves of ecstasy rippling through my nerve endings. I'm lost to the sensations, drowning in a sea of lust and need as he takes me higher, harder.

"You're mine," Ronan snarls, his fingers digging into my hips hard enough to bruise. He punctuates each word with a sharp snap of his hips. "This tight little cunt was made for my cock. Say it, Eliza. Tell me who you belong to."

"You," I sob, too far gone to deny him anything. "I'm yours, Ronan. Only yours."

His lips crash down on mine, swallowing my cries as he pistons into me with wild abandon. I can feel my climax building, fast and fierce, threatening to consume me. Ronan must sense it too because he slips a hand between us, his clever fingers finding my swollen nub.

He rubs tight circles around my clit, the dual stimulation hurtling me towards the edge. "Come," he commands, his voice a dark whisper against my ear. "Squeeze my cock like the greedy little thing you are."

I shatter on a scream, my walls clamping down on his rigid length as wave after wave of ecstasy crashes over me. Ronan growls, his hips stuttering as my orgasm triggers his own. He buries his face in the crook of my neck, sinking his teeth into the tender flesh as he emptied himself inside me.

I feel each hot spurt of his seed painting my inner walls, marking me as his. He comes like a man possessed, his cock pulsing and twitching with the force of his release. It seems to go on forever, his spend leaking out of me to pool on the sheets below.

Finally, he stills, his harsh breaths mingling with my own in the charged air. Ronan rolls off me, flopping onto his back as we both struggle to regain our bearings. I'm boneless, thoroughly used in the most delicious way. Every inch of my body hums with satisfaction, sated in a way I've never known.

I chance a glance at Ronan, taking in his disheveled hair and the sheen of sweat glistening on his golden skin. His expression is inscrutable, but there's a new intimacy in the way his eyes roam over my naked form, admiring the marks he's left behind.

Slowly, almost hesitantly, he reaches out to brush a damp strand of hair from my cheek. The tenderness in the gesture makes my heart clench.

I almost expect him to demand me to leave, but instead, he wraps a strong arm around me and pulls me to lay on his chest.

He doesn't speak, and I don't either. We just lay there together until I feel the even breathing of him drifting off to sleep.

And I lay there, pondering the enigma that is Ronan Black.

CHAPTER 5

hold my breath as I turn the key in the lock, the click echoing in the silent hall. I glance over my shoulder. Ronan is still fast asleep in his bed, but when I spotted the key on his nightstand, I couldn't resist. I had to investigate. I need to know what he's hiding.

The door swings open with a creak, revealing a dimly lit study. Rich mahogany shelves line the walls, filled with leather-bound tomes. A large oak desk dominates the center of the room, its surface covered in a scattering of papers.

My curiosity propels me forward, bare feet sinking into the plush Persian rug. The musty scent of old books mingles with the faint aroma of pipe tobacco as I trail my fingers along the smooth wood grain. Ronan's absence emboldens me to prowl deeper, to uncover the secrets he guards so fiercely.

I settle into the high-backed leather chair, the cool material sending a shiver down my spine. Fingers trembling slightly, I slide open the top drawer. Inside lies a stack of old photographs, their edges worn and yellowed with age. I lift them out gingerly, as if they might crumble to dust in my hands.

The top photo shows a younger Ronan, eyes hard and jaw set, standing with a group of rough-looking men. They exude an aura of danger, of violence barely contained. I flip through more images—Ronan shaking hands with shadowy figures, money exchanging hands under dim street lights, guns glinting at his hip.

My heart pounds in my ears as the pieces fall into place. The reclusive artist is a facade, a mask hiding a criminal past. Questions swirl in my mind—what exactly was he involved in? Is he still entangled in that dangerous world?

I startle at a shadow falling across the desk, the photos fluttering from my hands. I look up slowly, green eyes meeting piercing blue, to find Ronan standing in the doorway, a dark expression on his chiseled face. The air crackles with tension as I realize I've stumbled onto a truth he never intended me to find. In this moment, I'm not sure if I should feel exhilarated...or terrified.

He stalks forward, muscles rippling beneath taut skin, raw power emanating from every inch of his naked form. In a flash, his hand is around my throat, not squeezing but holding me firmly in place. I'm trapped, pinned by his stormy gaze as much as his unyielding grip.

"Are you happy now, little girl?" Ronan growls, his breath hot against my face. "Now that you've uncovered the monster lurking beneath the surface?"

I swallow hard against his palm, pulse fluttering wildly. Fear and a traitorous thrill course through my veins, igniting every nerve ending. I force myself to hold his stare, even as I tremble under the intensity.

"Monster? I don't..." The words lodge in my throat, confusion warring with a desperate need to understand the enigmatic man before me.

His lips twist into a cruel mockery of a smile. "Don't play coy. You saw the evidence of my sins. The blood staining my hands."

"Then explain it to me," I challenge, summoning a bravery I don't quite feel. "Make me understand…"

I trail off, unable to voice the accusations lingering between us. Ronan's fingers flex against my throat, his jaw clenching as he wars with some internal debate. The air grows heavy, charged with unspoken secrets and a simmering tension that threatens to ignite.

"You don't know what you're asking," he warns, his tone low and dangerous. "Once you see the darkness, there's no coming back from it."

But I refuse to back down, even as his touch brands my skin and his nearness overwhelms my senses. I need to know the truth, no matter how ugly or painful.

Ronan's gaze bores into mine, the icy blue of his eyes searing through the layers of my defenses. His hand remains at my throat, a silent reminder of the power he wields over me. The seconds stretch into an eternity as I wait for him to speak, my heart pounding a frantic rhythm against my ribs.

"I've killed people," he confesses, his voice rough with barely contained emotion. "More than I can count. It's all I've ever known, growing up in a world where violence was the only language spoken."

The admission hangs heavy in the air between us, a dark secret finally brought to light. I should feel horror, revulsion, but instead, a strange sense of understanding washes over me. The pieces of the puzzle that is Ronan Black slowly begin to fall into place.

"But why are you here, then?" I press, my voice barely above a whisper. "Why hide away in this remote cabin if you're the monster you claim to be?"

Ronan's grip on my throat loosens, his touch becoming almost gentle as his thumb traces the delicate line of my jaw. The contrast sends a shiver down my spine, desire mingling with the ever-present danger.

"I'm trying to escape it all," he murmurs, his gaze distant, as if seeing beyond the present moment. "The violence, the darkness that's consumed me for so long. I thought if I could just disappear, I could leave it all behind."

In that moment, I see beneath the facade he's so carefully constructed. The brooding artist, the enigmatic recluse...they're all masks he wears to hide the wounded man beneath. A man desperately seeking redemption, even if he believes himself unworthy of it.

My hand rises to cover his, our fingers intertwining against the warmth of my skin. The touch is electric, igniting a fire in my veins that threatens to consume me whole. I know I'm treading on dangerous ground, but I can't bring myself to pull away.

"You're not a monster, Ronan," I breathe, my words a whispered promise in the space between us. "You're a man haunted by his past, searching for a way out of the shadows."

His eyes flicker with an emotion I can't quite decipher—a mix of longing, desperation, and something darker, more primal. The air grows thick with tension, the silence broken only by the ragged sound of our breaths.

And then, without warning, he closes the distance between us, his lips crashing against mine in a bruising kiss that steals the air from my lungs. I'm lost in the taste of him, the feel of his body pressed against mine, the world falling away until there's nothing left but this moment, this connection, this all-consuming need.

Ronan's hands roam over my body with a possessive urgency, his touch both demanding and reverent. His fingers tangle in my hair, tugging just hard enough to send a shiver down my spine as he deepens the kiss, claiming my mouth with a fervor that borders on desperation.

We stumble backwards, a tangle of limbs and racing heartbeats, until my back hits the wall with a dull thud. Ronan's body presses against mine, the heat of his skin searing through the thin fabric of my shirt. His lips trail down the column of my throat, teeth grazing the sensitive skin, marking me as his own.

A gasp escapes my lips as his hands slip beneath my shirt, calloused fingers skimming over my ribcage, my stomach, leaving trails of fire in their wake. My own hands explore the planes of his back, nails digging into his flesh as I try to anchor myself in the maelstrom of sensations threatening to sweep me away.

He tears my shirt off with a growl, the sound reverberating through my bones, igniting a primal hunger deep within me. Our eyes lock, blue on green, a silent conversation passing between us—a question, a plea, a promise.

And then, we're moving again, a frenzied dance of tangled limbs and discarded clothing, until there's nothing left between us but skin on skin, the heat of our bodies merging into one. Ronan's hands grip my thighs, lifting me effortlessly as I wrap my legs around his waist, the evidence of his arousal pressing insistently against my core.

He enters me in one swift, powerful thrust, filling me so completely that I can't tell where I end and he begins. A cry of pleasure tears from my throat as he begins to move, each stroke deeper, harder, more demanding than the last.

His hand finds its way to my throat, fingers tightening ever so slightly, the pressure a delicious mix of danger and ecstasy. My breath comes in shallow gasps as he drives into me relentlessly, his eyes never leaving mine, a silent challenge, a wordless command to surrender everything to him.

The coil of tension in my belly winds tighter and tighter, my body trembling on the brink of something vast and all-consuming. Ronan's grip on my throat tightens, his thrusts becoming more erratic, more desperate, until finally, with a hoarse cry, he releases me, sending me spiraling over the edge into a shattering climax that rips through my body like a tidal wave.

I cling to him as he finds his own release, his body shuddering against mine, a guttural groan echoing in the stillness of the room. For a long moment, we remain locked in an embrace, our hearts pounding in sync, our breaths mingling in the charged air between us.

As the world slowly comes back into focus, I'm left with the unshakable feeling that something has irrevocably shifted between us—a line crossed, a boundary shattered, a path chosen from which there can be no turning back.

And yet, even as the weight of that realization settles heavily upon my chest, I know with a bone-deep certainty that I wouldn't have it any other way.

"Ronan," I begin, my voice a raspy whisper, my fingers tentatively stroking his damp hair. "I—"

"You can never leave here now." His voice is a low growl, cutting me off mid-sentence.

I freeze.

"You know my deepest secrets," his eyes bore into mine with a look that borders on madness. "You are mine now."

Ronan's words send a chill down my spine, even as a dark thrill coils in my belly. His eyes are fathomless pools of blue, swirling with a dangerous intensity that threatens to consume me whole.

"You don't understand," he growls, his breath hot against my skin. "I'm not a good man, Eliza. I'm possessive, obsessive. Once I claim something as mine, I never let it go."

His hand tightens on my throat, a silent reminder of his dominance, his control. I should be terrified, but instead, a perverse excitement thrums through my veins. There's a dark allure to being wanted so fiercely, so completely.

"I won't let you expose me," Ronan continues, his lips brushing the shell of my ear. "I can't risk you revealing my secrets, my whereabouts. From this moment on, you belong to me. Body, mind, and soul."

A shudder runs through me at his declaration, desire warring with trepidation. To be owned so thoroughly, to surrender myself to this enigmatic, dangerous man—it's as thrilling as it is terrifying.

"And what if I don't want to be trapped?" I breathe, testing the limits of his control, even as I arch into his unyielding grip.

A dark chuckle rumbles through his chest, the sound raising goosebumps on my flesh.

"Oh, my sweet Eliza," he murmurs, his tone a silken caress laced with warning. "then you shouldn't have walked into the lion's den."

His mouth claims mine once more, the kiss a searing brand of possession that steals the air from my lungs. I'm lost in the taste of him, the feel of his hard body pressed against mine, the intoxicating mix of danger and desire that clouds my senses.

When he finally pulls back, his eyes are dark with promise, with a hunger that threatens to devour me whole. "You're mine now," he repeats, each word a solemn vow. "And I protect what's mine, even if it means keeping you locked away from the world forever."

A part of me knows I should be frightened by his intensity, his unyielding need to possess me so completely. But another part, a secret, shameful part, thrills at the idea of being his, of surrendering to the dark passions he stirs within me.

"But don't worry," he murmurs against my neck, "I will keep you so exhausted with pleasure that you won't even have the energy to focus on escaping."

As Ronan's hands roam over my body, his touch a searing brand of ownership, I realize that I'm already lost, already ensnared in his web of seduction and danger. And despite the warning bells clanging in my mind, I can't bring myself to fight it.

Because deep down, in a hidden corner of my soul, I crave the very darkness he embodies. I yearn to lose myself in his shadows, to be consumed by the flames of his obsession.

CHAPTER 6

The storm rages outside my window, winds howling like a wounded beast as sheets of rain lash against the glass. I watch, transfixed by the chaotic dance of the elements, my own thoughts a tempest within. Ronan. His name echoes through my mind, a whisper and a shout all at once. The intensity of our connection, the way he unravels me with a single glance, both thrills and terrifies me.

I wrap my arms around myself, as if to contain the unfamiliar feelings threatening to overflow. *Submission.* The word tastes foreign on my tongue, yet it calls to me like a siren's song. With Ronan, I find myself yearning to surrender, to let go of the iron-clad control I've clung to for so long. But fear lurks in the shadows of my desire, a cold reminder of the vulnerability that comes with relinquishing power.

The flickering firelight casts dancing shadows on the walls, mirroring the push and pull within my heart. I am drawn to Ronan in ways I cannot fully comprehend, my curiosity a relentless force urging me to explore the depths of this connection. Yet a part of me hesitates, wary of the unknown territory that lies ahead.

I should be angry he's effectively kidnapped me.

But I'm not.

Is something wrong with me?

I lean my forehead against the cool glass, letting the chill seep into my skin. The storm's fury seems to mirror the turmoil within, a physical manifestation of the emotions I struggle to untangle. Ronan's presence looms large in my mind, his piercing blue eyes haunting my thoughts. I can almost feel the weight of his gaze upon me, the unspoken promises and uncharted desires that hang heavy in the air between us.

As the wind howls and the rain beats a staccato rhythm against the window pane, I close my eyes and surrender to the maelstrom within. The yearning to understand, to dive headfirst into the intoxicating dance of dominance and submission, consumes me. Fear and curiosity intertwine, a heady cocktail that sets my nerves alight with anticipation.

In the solitude of this moment, I allow myself to imagine the possibilities, to dare to dream of a world where I can let go and embrace the freedom found in submission. The thought is both exhilarating and terrifying, a leap into the unknown that promises to shatter the carefully constructed walls I've built around my heart.

The door creaks open, and my heart leaps into my throat. I don't need to turn around to know it's him. Ronan's presence fills the room, a tangible force that seems to command the very air we breathe. I feel his gaze upon me, a searing heat that ignites a fire beneath my skin, and I'm suddenly acutely aware of every inch of my body.

I inhale deeply, trying to steady myself, but his scent envelops me—a heady mix of citrus, pine, and something uniquely him. It's intoxicating, and I find myself fighting the urge to lean into it, to drown in the essence of him.

Ronan moves with a deliberate grace, his

footsteps barely audible over the raging storm outside. Each step he takes towards me feels like an eternity, a slow, tortuous dance that sets my nerves alight with anticipation. I grip the windowsill, my knuckles turning white as I try to anchor myself against the onslaught of sensations.

He stands beside me now, close enough that I can feel the heat radiating from his body. We both stare out into the tempest, the silence between us thick with unspoken words and shared awareness. It's as if the snowstorm outside is a mere reflection of the one brewing within us, a whirlwind of desire, fear, and the tantalizing promise of something more.

I risk a glance at him from the corner of my eye, taking in the sharp angles of his jaw, the way his dark hair falls across his brow. There's a tension in his posture, a coiled energy that speaks of restraint and barely contained passion. It's mesmerizing, and I find myself wanting to unravel the mystery that is Ronan Black.

The air crackles with electricity, and I'm acutely aware of every breath I take, every shift of his body next to mine. It's a delicious torment, this unspoken connection that pulls us together like two magnets, inevitable and irresistible.

In this moment, the rest of the world falls away, and there is only us—two souls caught in the eye of the storm, teetering on the brink of something profound and life-altering. The silence stretches on, a heavy, tangible thing, and I know that when it finally breaks, nothing will ever be the same again.

"What do you see when you look out there, Eliza?" Ronan's voice, low and measured, breaks the silence, sending a shiver down my spine. There's a weight to his words, a hidden depth that I long to explore.

I swallow, my throat suddenly dry. "Chaos," I whisper, my gaze fixed on the swirling tempest beyond the glass. "A force of nature that can't be tamed or controlled."

Ronan hums, a sound that resonates deep within his chest. "And what about our current predicament? Do you feel the same way about that?"

I turn to face him, my heart hammering against my ribcage. His eyes, those piercing blue orbs, seem to see straight through me, unraveling the layers of my soul. "I don't know," I admit, my voice barely above a whisper. "There's something about you, about this, that both terrifies and intrigues me."

A ghost of a smile plays at the corner of his lips, and he reaches out, his fingers brushing against my cheek with a gentleness that belies the intensity of his gaze. "You don't hate me for keeping you here?"

His touch ignites a fire within me, a yearning that I've never experienced before. It's as if his fingers leave a trail of electricity in their wake, awakening parts of me that I never knew existed. I lean into his touch, my eyes fluttering closed for a brief moment, savoring the sensation.

"I don't know," I whisper, my voice trembling with a mix of anticipation and fear.

Ronan's hand lingers on my face, his thumb tracing the outline of my lower lip. It's a possessive gesture, one that speaks of a deeper connection, a claim that he's staking on my very being. I feel myself falling under his spell, drawn to him like a moth to a flame.

"You're perfect, Eliza," he murmurs, his breath warm against my skin.

I meet his gaze, my own resolve hardening. "If I want to leave, I will."

His eyes darken, a storm of their own

brewing within their depths. "We'll see about that," he whispers, his words a promise and a challenge all at once.

And with that, he closes the distance between us, his lips claiming mine in a searing kiss that steals the very breath from my lungs.

A shiver runs down my spine as Ronan's lips move against mine, demanding and unyielding. His touch ignites a fire within me, a desire that threatens to consume me whole. I find myself losing all sense of reason, all thought of resistance, as I melt into his embrace.

But as quickly as it began, the kiss ends, leaving me breathless and aching for more. Ronan pulls back, his eyes searching mine, a flicker of uncertainty crossing his face. It's a rare glimpse of vulnerability, a crack in his carefully crafted facade.

The silence stretches between us, heavy with unspoken words and the weight of our shared desire. The storm outside rages on, the wind howling like a tortured soul, the sleeting rain pounding against the window like a relentless drumbeat. It's as if the very elements are reflecting the turmoil within us, the push and pull of our conflicting emotions.

I find myself torn, caught between the desire

to surrender to this all-consuming passion and the fear of losing myself completely. Ronan's touch has awakened something within me, a part of myself that I never knew existed, a part that craves his dominance, his control.

But at the same time, I can feel my independence slipping away, my sense of self being subsumed by his overwhelming presence. It's a terrifying realization, one that forces me to confront the boundaries I've so carefully constructed around my heart.

The silence stretches on, the only sound the relentless pounding of the storm against the window panes. Ronan's gaze never wavers from mine, his eyes a storm of their own, dark and turbulent with barely restrained passion.

"What are you thinking?" he asks, his voice low and rough, breaking the spell of the moment.

I swallow hard, struggling to find the words to express the maelstrom of emotions swirling within me. "I'm thinking that I'm in over my head," I whisper, my voice trembling with a mix of fear and desire. "That I'm not sure I can handle this, handle you."

Ronan's hand comes up to cup my face, his touch gentle yet possessive. "You're stronger than you know, Eliza," he murmurs, his thumb tracing the curve of my cheekbone. "Trust me to guide you, to show you the depths of your own desire."

I lean into his touch, my eyes fluttering closed, my breath coming in shallow gasps. I want to trust him, to surrender myself completely to his will. But a part of me still hesitates, still clings to the last vestiges of my independence.

"I'm afraid," I confess, my voice barely above a whisper. "Afraid of losing myself in you."

Ronan's lips curve into a smile, a rare sight that sends a thrill down my spine. "Don't be afraid, Eliza," he whispers, his breath warm against my skin. "My obsession with you can be a gratifying experience for you. Embrace the fear, the uncertainty. Let it fuel your desire, your passion. Let me show you the beauty in surrender."

And with those words, he claims my lips once more, his kiss a searing promise of the pleasure and pain to come.

As he continues to devour my mouht, Ronan's touches become bolder, his caresses more assertive. He unbuttons my blouse one agonizingly slow button at a time, revealing the lacy black bra beneath. His eyes darken, filled with desire and control, as he traces his fingertips along the delicate fabric.

"You're mine," he growls, his voice a low rumble that sends shivers down my spine. "Body, mind, and soul. You belong to me, Eliza. Say it."

I shiver at his possessive declaration, a defiant spark igniting within me. "I belong to no one," I retort, my voice steady despite the pounding of my heart. "Not even you."

Ronan's eyes flash with a dangerous glint, a predatory smile curving his lips. "Is that so?" he purrs, his fingers tightening on my chin. "We'll see about that."

In one swift motion, he spins me around and pulls me down across his lap. I gasp, disoriented by the sudden change in position. My blouse hangs open, my breasts spilling out of my bra. I feel exposed, vulnerable, as Ronan's strong hands pin me in place.

"Let me go!" I demand, struggling against his iron grip. But deep down, a traitorous part of me thrills at his show of dominance.

"I don't think so," Ronan growls. "Not until you learn your place."

His hand comes down on my backside with a sharp smack, the sting radiating through my thin skirt. I cry out, more from shock than pain. He spanks me again, harder this time, and I bite my lip to stifle a moan.

"You will submit to me, Eliza," he commands, punctuating each word with another firm swat. "You will surrender that stubborn will of yours and accept that you are mine."

Tears prick my eyes as he continues the relentless onslaught, my bottom growing hot and tender under his punishing hand. Shame and humiliation bubble up within me. Each slap of his palm against my sensitive flesh sends a jolt straight to my core, stoking the embers of my arousal.

I writhe across his lap, torn between the urge to escape and the dark desire to submit to his will. "Please," I gasp, unsure if I'm begging him to stop or to never stop. "Please, Ronan..."

"Please, what?" he demands, his voice a low, dangerous purr. "Please spank you harder? Please make you admit that you belong to me?"

"No!" I sob, hot tears spilling down my cheeks. But even as I deny him, I feel my resistance crumbling, my body betraying my need.

Ronan's hand cracks down again, the hardest yet, and I can't help but moan as the pain blossoms into perverse pleasure. "You will yield to me," he growls, his breath hot against my ear. "Say it, Eliza. Say that you're mine."

With one final, searing smack, I break. "I'm yours!" I cry out, going limp over his lap as the fight drains out of me. "I belong to you, Ronan. Only you."

He pulls me up into his arms, cradling my trembling body against his chest. "Good girl," he praises, his lips brushing my tear-stained cheek.

Ronan's fingers slip beneath my skirt, caressing my throbbing, heated flesh through the damp lace of my panties. I gasp and arch into his touch, the intensity of my need overriding any lingering shame or resistance.

"So wet for me already," he purrs approvingly, tracing teasing circles that make me writhe and whimper with desperation. "Your body knows who it belongs to, even if your stubborn mind still fights it."

Without warning, he yanks my panties aside and plunges two thick fingers deep inside me. A guttural moan escapes my lips at the sudden invasion, my slick walls clenching greedily around him. He pumps into my aching core with ruthless skill, hitting that secret spot that makes stars explode behind my eyelids.

"That's it, my sweet Eliza," Ronan growls, curling his fingers in a 'come hither' motion that has me seeing galaxies. "Ride my hand. Show me how much you need my touch."

Wantonly, I grind myself against his thrusting digits, chasing the devastating plea-sure only he can give me. The obscene sound of my wetness fills the room as he finger-fucks me hard and deep. My head thrashes and my thighs quiver uncontrollably. I'm so close already, balanced on the razor's edge of rapture.

"Please," I keen helplessly, too far gone to care how desperate I sound. "Please, I need...I need..."

"I know exactly what you need," Ronan rasps, his voice dark with lust and satisfaction. "And I'm going to give it to you. Come for me, Eliza. Now."

His command slices through me like a light-ning bolt, and I detonate. My orgasm crashes over me in a tidal wave of sensation, stealing my breath and obliterating my thoughts. I spasm and clench wildly on his fingers, gushing my release as I shatter apart with a ragged scream.

Ronan works me through the aftershocks, his touch gentling as I slowly float back down to earth. Overwhelming emotions surge through me—the intensity of my climax, the vulnerability of my submission, the soul-deep connection I feel to this complicated, captivating man.

Suddenly, I burst into raw, body-wracking sobs, unable to hold back the flood any longer. Ronan gathers me tenderly into his arms, cradling me against his strong chest as I weep. He strokes my hair and murmurs soothing words of praise and reassurance.

"Shh, it's alright, sweet girl. You're safe. You were perfect, so good for me. Let it all out, I've got you," he croons, rocking me gently.

Bit by bit, enfolded in his solid strength and care, my tears subside.

"You were made for this," he whispers. "Made to be my obsession, and I'm going to worship you with every twisted bone in my body," he vows.

CHAPTER 7

The crackling fire casts dancing shadows across Ronan's enigmatic face as we sit together on the plush rug, sipping mulled wine. Outside, snow blankets the world in hushed stillness, but inside the air is charged with unspoken questions.

"Your family," Ronan says, his deep voice barely rising above the snapping logs. "Won't they miss you this Christmas Eve?"

I stare into the flickering flames, the heat searing my cheeks. "I have no family." The words leave a bitter aftertaste on my tongue.

Silence stretches between us, broken only by the pop and hiss of the fire. I feel Ronan's penetrating gaze on me, as if trying to peel back the layers of my soul and glimpse the truth buried there.

He leans in closer, the spiced scent of the wine on his breath. "What happened to you, Eliza?" His question is soft, almost tender, belying the intensity in his ice-blue eyes.

My heartbeat quickens and I take a shaky sip of wine, the warm liquid sliding down my throat. Can he see the cracks in my carefully constructed facade? The painful secrets I've buried deep?

I avoid his probing stare and watch the fire instead, mesmerized by the undulating flames. They seem to beckon me, whispering of a release from the memories that haunt me. But I remain silent, trapped between the desperate need to unburden myself and the fear of revealing too much.

Ronan's fingers brush my arm, his touch electric even through the thick wool of my sweater. "Tell me," he murmurs, his voice a soothing balm.

My throat closes up, and I close my eyes. I don't like to think about it.

The memories…

Outside, the wind picks up, rattling the frosted windowpanes with a mournful howl.

The shadows in the room lengthen, reaching out like grasping fingers. And still, Ronan waits patiently for an answer I'm not ready to give.

When I finally speak, my voice is barely a whisper. "It's a long story," I say, hoping he'll drop it.

Ronan's expression doesn't change, but I catch the flicker of determination in his eyes. "We have all night," he says simply, refilling my wineglass.

Tension swirls between us like the swirling snowflakes outside. The fire crackles menacingly, as if it knows the secrets I'm desperate to keep hidden.

Ronan's fingers graze the rope coiled on the mantelpiece, and I shiver, my entire body tensing up. He smirks, as if he can read my thoughts. "I can be...persuasive, when I need to be."

The air thickens with anticipation and dread, the room pulsing with an erotic charge I can't deny. Part of me is terrified, but a much darker, unexplored part of me thrills at the prospect of giving up control.

I shake my head.

Ronan's eyes darken, a hunger I've never seen before flashing in their depths. He stands and pulls me to my feet. "What happened to you, Eliza?" he asks, his voice low and gravelly.

I takes a shaky breath, fighting to keep the memories at bay. But they're like the relentless tide, crashing over me, dragging me under.

"It was a few years ago," I begin, my stomach churning with revulsion. "I was working on a story, an exposé on human trafficking. I...thought I could handle it. But I was wrong."

Ronan's hands are firm but steady as he guides me to the bedroom. He blindfolds me, binding my wrists above my head. I'm helpless, at his mercy or mercilessness.

"Tell me everything," he growls, his voice dark and demanding.

I resist, and then I feel the sting of his hand on my ass.

Still, I don't speak.

He spanks me again. Harder.

Again and again, he strikes me. I feel his hard cock press against me, evidence of how much this is turning him on.

Wetness pools between my thighs, evidence of my own desire.

"Tell me, Eliza!" he roars.

Then, he thrusts his cock into me, and I break.

Something shifts inside me, a dam breaking under the weight of his relentless pursuit. Tears sting my eyes as the truth claws its way up my throat, demanding release. "I...I was..." The words catch, lodged in a web of pain and shame.

Ronan's hand cups my cheek, his thumb brushing away the lone tear that escapes. "Let it out, Eliza. I've got you."

And so, in halting phrases punctuated by shuddering breaths, I reveal my darkest secret. The night that shattered me, leaving jagged scars on my soul. "They...they took turns... all three of them. I couldn't...I couldn't stop it..."

A sob wrenches from my chest as the memories assault me. The cruel laughter, the bruising grips, the searing pain. I'm drowning in it, gasping for air.

He pulls his cock free as everything comes pouring out of me in a torrent. I tell him about the night I was lured to a remote location, how three men ambushed me in a dark alley. The way they'd laughed as they'd torn away my clothes, my pride, and my innocence. The way they'd violated me, one after another, their laughter and taunts echoing in my mind like a never-ending nightmare.

My entire body is trembling, and then I feel Ronan reenter me, gently this time.

He unties me and removes the blindfold, his eyes angrier than I've ever seen them. "I'll kill them. I'll hunt them down and kill them."

I close my eyes.

"Look at me," he demands. "I've got you, baby. You're safe. No one will ever hurt you again. I swear it. You're mine now, princess."

I cling to him, my face buried against his chest. His heartbeat thunders beneath my cheek, a war drum heralding retribution. And in that moment, I surrender myself completely to his strength, him

No more fighting it.

I am his.

CHAPTER 8

The snow falls in heavy flakes outside the frosted cabin window, blanketing the world in suffocating silence. I stare out at the endless expanse of white, my heart pounding with a growing unease. Ronan's words echo in my mind, carving themselves into my very being. *You're mine, Eliza. I will never let you leave.*

His strong arms wrap around my waist from behind, his breath hot against my ear. "Don't fight it anymore. We both know this is where you belong."

I close my eyes, leaning back into his solid warmth despite myself. The rational part of me screams that this is madness, that I should run as far and fast as I can. But a deeper, primal instinct whispers that Ronan is right—that everything I've ever wanted is right here in his embrace.

My voice trembles as I whisper, "I don't know who I am anymore. How can I want this so desperately when it goes against everything I thought I believed in?"

Ronan turns me to face him, his piercing blue eyes boring into my soul. "Because we are the same, you and I. Two broken pieces that fit together perfectly. The world out there will never understand the depth of what we share."

I gaze up at him, my fingers tracing the chiseled lines of his jaw. The intensity of my emotions terrifies and exhilarates me in equal measure. I know I should push him away, but I'm drowning in the magnetic pull between us.

Snowflakes swirl hypnotically beyond the glass, and a heavy certainty settles over me, smothering the last of my doubts. There is no going back from this—from him.

"Nothing is waiting for me out there," I murmur, almost to myself.

A slow smile spreads across Ronan's face, equal parts triumph and relief. He pulls me flush against him, his lips claiming mine in a searing kiss that sets my blood on fire.

As I melt into him, I finally accept the inescapable truth—I am irrevocably his...and a part of me has longed for this surrender all along.

The world beyond the cabin fades away until there is only Ronan, our ragged breaths mingling as the storm rages on outside.

The passion between us boils over, spilling into a desperate, consuming fire that cannot be contained. We cling to each other as if we might evaporate if we let go. Our clothes are discarded, discarded pieces of armor shedding away, leaving us bare in more ways than one.

Ronan's hands roam the curves of my body, every touch a living flame that ignites new lust within me. His mouth is hot on my skin, leaving a trail of fire in its wake. I've never felt more alive or more desired than in this moment.

We fall together onto the four-poster bed, our bodies entwined, and I fight to catch my breath in the delicious intensity of it all. The flames in the fireplace dance in time with our frenzied movements, casting twisted shadows upon the wall.

"Say it," Ronan growls, his voice guttural as he presses me further into the mattress. "Say you're mine, Eliza."

"I'm yours," I gasp, my nails raking down his back as the world narrows to him—only him. "Yours, Ronan."

A shuddering mo an is torn from his lips, and I feel his need pulsing against me, a testament to his desire. He penetrates me slowly, as if savoring every second of our union.

"God, Eliza," he moans, burying his face in the crook of my neck, "I want to break you and put you back together again."

His words unravel me further, and I arch my hips up against his, urging him to take me deeper. He obliges, thrusting deep within me with a growl that sets my blood on fire.

Our bodies move in rhythm, our harsh breaths mingling with the howling wind outside.

"I won't let anyone hurt you again," he whispers fiercely, his blue eyes blazing into mine, "I promise, Eliza. I'll protect you—always."

The truth in his words is my undoing, and I climax, crying out his name as the world explodes around us.

———

One year later

I stand before the frost-kissed windowpane, my hands pressed against the icy glass as I stare out at the snow-covered manor grounds. It's Christmas Eve again, and the outdoors has been transformed into a snowy abyss again— much like last year when I first got stranded here.

A warmth blooms in my chest as I think back on the past year. All the dominance and submission. The deliciously twisted games Ronan and I play.

I feel strong arms encircle my waist from behind, and I turn, delighted to see that Ronan is finally back. He left a few days ago without telling me where he was going.

I fling my arms around Ronan's neck, pulling him close as our lips meet in a searing kiss. The chill from the window melts away as his warmth envelops me, his strong hands splaying across my back. When we finally break apart, I search his face, my fingers tracing the sharp angles of his jaw.

"Where have you been?" I whisper, my voice

laced with a mixture of relief and curiosity. "I was worried."

Ronan's piercing blue eyes bore into mine, a flicker of something dark and dangerous dancing within their depths. He takes a deep breath, as if steeling himself for what he's about to say.

"I found them, Eliza," he says quietly, his tone laced with a barely restrained fury. "The men who hurt you. I killed them. Slowly. Painfully. Making sure they knew my fury."

My heart stutters in my chest as the weight of his words sinks in. A part of me knows I should be horrified, but instead, a strange sense of relief washes over me. The shadows of my past that have haunted me for so long suddenly feel lighter, as if Ronan has taken on the burden himself.

Tears prick at the corners of my eyes, and I cup his face in my hands. "You...you did that for me?"

He nods, his gaze never wavering from mine. "I promised I would protect you, Eliza. I meant it. And I will always avenge you."

Emotion swells within me, a tidal wave of love and gratitude that threatens to sweep me away. I press my forehead against his, our breaths mingling in the charged space between us.

"Thank you," I whisper, pouring every ounce of my heart into those two simple words.

Ronan's hands slide down to my hips, pulling me flush against him. "There's something else," he murmurs, his voice low and rough with emotion.

Slowly, he steps back and begins to unbutton his shirt. My breath catches in my throat as he reveals his chest, inch by tantalizing inch. And there, right over his heart, is a tattoo of my name in elegant script.

My fingers tremble as I reach out to trace the inked lines, marveling at the permanence of it—of us. Ronan's hand covers mine, pressing it flat against his skin. I can feel the steady thrum of his heartbeat beneath my palm.

"I'm more than in love with you, Eliza," he says, his voice a raw, guttural whisper. "I'm utterly, irrevocably obsessed with you. You're in my veins, in every fiber of my being. I will never let you go."

His words ignite a fire within me, and I surge forward, capturing his lips in a desperate, consuming kiss. We stumble backwards until my back hits the wall,

Ronan's body presses against mine, pinning me to the wall as our kiss deepens. His hands roam my curves with a possessive urgency that sets my skin ablaze. I can feel the evidence of his arousal straining against his trousers, and I grind my hips against him, eliciting a low growl from the back of his throat.

"You drive me fucking crazy, Eliza," he rasps, his lips trailing down the column of my neck. "I need you. Now."

With a swift movement, he rips open my blouse, sending buttons scattering across the hardwood floor. Cool air kisses my exposed skin, but it's quickly replaced by the searing heat of Ronan's mouth as he lavishes attention on my breasts.

I tangle my fingers in his dark hair, holding him closer as pleasure coils tightly in my core. "Then take me," I breathe, my voice barely above a whisper. "I'm yours, Ronan. Completely."

A primal hunger flares in his eyes, and he lifts me effortlessly, carrying me to the plush rug before the crackling fireplace. He lays me down with a gentleness that belies the intensity of his desire, his hands skimming reverently over my body as he divests me of the rest of my clothing.

"You're so fucking beautiful," he murmurs, his gaze drinking me in like a man starved. "I'll never get enough of you."

He quickly sheds his own clothes before settling between my thighs, his hardness pressing insistently against my slick entrance. With a powerful thrust, he sheaths himself fully inside me, and I cry out at the exquisite stretch of my body accommodating his.

Ronan sets a relentless pace, driving into me with deep, purposeful strokes that send shock-waves of ecstasy rippling through my veins. The firelight dances across his chiseled features, casting him in an ethereal glow that steals my breath away.

"Look at me, Eliza," he commands, his voice rough with need. "I want to see you fall apart for me."

I meet his penetrating gaze, my walls clenching around him as I teeter on the precipice of oblivion. "Ronan, please..."

"That's it, baby," he encourages, his thrusts growing more erratic as he chases his own release. "Come for me. Let me feel you."

His words are my undoing, and I shatter

beneath him, my back arching off the rug as wave after wave of mind-numbing pleasure crashes over me. Ronan follows me over the edge with a guttural moan, spilling himself deep inside me as he buries his face in the crook of my neck.

We cling to each other in the aftermath, our bodies slick with sweat and the evidence of our passion.

And I know that this is where I'm meant to be.

Trapped here with him today and for every Christmas to come.

Want more? Go to www.spicy-romance.com for a free book!

Keep reading for an excerpt from Cruel Master:

Chapter 1

I will not cry.

I will not cry.

Tears begin streaming down my cheeks.

Fuck, I'm crying.

But, damn it, how could I not?

I scream into my gag and writhe, my body flopping back and forth across the floor of the dirty van. The floor feels sticky against my legs, and I don't even want to contemplate what's contributing to that slimy texture. My hands are bound painfully behind my back, and my ankles are tied together too.

It's as cold as an icebox in here, and I'm freezing in my cut-off jean shorts and flimsy little tank top. My nipples pebble painfully, and goosebumps break out on my flesh.

I squeeze my eyes shut and focus on breathing in and out through my nose. It's hard to engage in meditative breathing when panic is making your chest so tight you feel like you're going to have a heart attack even though you're only nineteen years old.

Only nineteen years old. Naïve. Stupid.

I should have known better. My sister and I have loved to binge-watch Lifetime movies ever since we were little girls. I should have seen it coming. It had all the makings of a kidnapping flick written all over it, yet I still took the bait like the desperate little fool I am.

When the photographer in the mall singled me out and told me I'd make a perfect model, I should have seen it coming.

I've seen this very scenario played out in countless movies on LMN, yet I still fell for it.

I believed I was different, that I was untouchable, that nothing so horrible as kidnapping could really happen to me. Is that how the other girls whom this has happened to felt?

I also wanted to believe that I really was pretty enough to be a model, that I could start making some real money and change things for my sister and me. No more working two dead-end jobs, scraping by from paycheck to paycheck. No more going to the local food banks just to make sure my little sister had enough food. I'm not college material, and even if I was, it takes money to go to school. Even if I'd gotten grants or scholarships, it takes money to live, especially when you have a kid sister to take care of.

My heart twists at the thought of Gia. My god, what will she do without me? She's only fifteen, too young to take care of herself, but I know my sister. She'll do everything she can to avoid going back into foster care. It was hell for us both. That's why as soon as I turned eighteen, I did everything I could to prove myself responsible so I could get custody of her.

I promised her we'd never be separated again, and now I'm being ripped from her.

What will she think happened to me? Surely, she'll know I didn't abandon her like our piece-of-shit mother. God, please don't let her end up on the streets. I've fought so hard to keep us both off them. I've seen too many of us foster kids end up there, chewed up and spat out by society. I don't want that for my baby sis.

Fresh tears rush to my eyes at the thought of my baby sis spiraling into a depression, thinking that the responsibility became too much for me and I bailed on her.

I flail again in frustration as sobs overtake me. My scream is muffled against the gag, but I have to let it out anyway.

The guy had sounded so legit. He had a business card and everything and gave me an official time and place to meet him for a test shoot.

As soon as I walked into the decrepit-looking old warehouse, I knew something was wrong. A shiver had run up my spine, and I'd turned to hightail it out of there, but it was already too late.

I felt the prick of the needle against my skin, and this is how I woke up.

Bound and gagged in the back of a dirty old van.

I try to be smart and take note of my surroundings, but it's so dark in here I can hardly make out anything. There's a sliver of light peaking in from the front where the driver sits, but there aren't any windows back here, of course, so I can't try to note any landmarks or street signs.

The light is flashing soft and yellow, though, like it does when you're driving down the street at night.

So, it's night. I don't know yet if that knowledge will help me or how, but I make note of it. It's nighttime. Maybe it will let me get a sense of time if nothing else.

I have to be smart. I think of all those real-life crime shows Gia and I watched together and how the girls who ended up escaping made note of everything they could even if they couldn't see anything.

I try to remember every turn we make and

time the minutes between each one. We turned left, then right after about two minutes, then right again after five? Then left again. No, wait, or was it right? And how much time has it been? There are sixty seconds in a minute, and I counted to three hundred fifty since last time...

Fuck this! I scream into my gag again in frustration. I'm not smart enough for this! I don't have a good enough memory for numbers on the best of days—much less when I'm bound and gagged like a critter soon to be roasted over a pit.

I lay there crying and breathing heavily as fear sluices through my veins. What's going to happen to me? Is he going to kill me? Rape me? Is he going to torture me?

I begin to shake uncontrollably when I remember all the crime documentaries I've seen and some of the horrible ways the people in them died.

Is this guy a serial killer? Is there any way I can reason with him when we eventually get to wherever he's taking me? Try to humanize yourself to the predator. That's what they always say on those shows.

I have to try to make him like me, try not to

show my fear because if it's fear he gets off on, then that's only going to amp him up.

Or, it might just piss him off if I don't react the way he wants me to.

More tears stream down my face at the helplessness of my situation. I don't know what to do. It's a gamble either way.

I close my eyes and think of Gia. I go through every good memory of my sister I have. Us playing together in the park. Her tenth birthday when I stole us both a pair of skates and snuck us into the skating rink. The day I officially adopted her.

Memories of my sister calm me as I remind myself that I have a reason to fight. I have my sister.

I begin trying to pay attention to any little details I can again. I'm not being jostled around as much anymore, so we're on a smoother road. A highway maybe? What kind of road were we on before then?

My heart begins hammering against my ribcage when my body sways forward as the brakes engage.

We're slowing down, coming to a stop.

Surely, we're not on a highway then. Probably a private drive then? A paved one?

The engine dies, and then I hear the slam of the door as someone gets out of the front. It sounded like it came from the passenger side, though—not the driver's side.

My stomach lurches. Does that mean there are two of them? One I have yet to see?

Oh god, being tortured and raped and killed by one monster is bad enough, but two?

Please don't let me be that unlucky, I pray to any deity out there that will listen.

The door opens, and I blink against the sudden, blinding light of a cell phone's flashlight shining right in my face.

"Alright, girl. Up we go," a voice I recognize as the photographer's from the mall speaks coldly.

He moves the flashlight up, and I look up at his goatee and bald head. He's big and muscular with a plain white T-shirt and low-slung jeans. Not exactly handsome but not hideous either. I'd thought he looked artistic back at the mall. He'd looked like a legitimate photographer in my mind, but now I see him for what he is.

A criminal.

He reaches in to grab me by the arms and haul me up, but when I see his big hands looming toward me, I forget everything I'd told myself I was going to do.

I act on pure instinct instead and twist onto my back until my feet are up in the air. The weight of my spine on my hands makes my wrists ache, but I ignore it.

I lift my bound feet and kick as hard as I can straight at the man's face.

Get Cruel Master here: Cruel Master.